'A *Wunderkind* –
a *Wunderkind* a
Wunderkind. The
syllables would
come out rolling in
the deep German
way, roar against
her ears and then
fall to a murmur…'

CARSON MCCULLERS
Born 19 February 1917, Columbus, Georgia
Died 29 September 1967, Nyack, New York

The stories included here were first published in book form
in *The Ballad of the Sad Café and Other Works* (1951).

ALSO PUBLISHED BY PENGUIN BOOKS
The Heart is a Lonely Hunter · *Reflections in a Golden Eye* ·
The Member of the Wedding · *The Ballad of the Sad Café* ·
Clock Without Hands · *The Mortgaged Heart*

CARSON MCCULLERS

Wunderkind

PENGUIN BOOKS

PENGUIN CLASSICS

Published by the Penguin Group
Penguin Books Ltd, 80 Strand, London WC2R ORL, England
Penguin Group (USA) Inc., 375 Hudson Street, New York, New York 10014, USA
Penguin Group (Canada), 90 Eglinton Avenue East, Suite 700, Toronto, Ontario,
Canada M4P 2Y3 (a division of Pearson Penguin Canada Inc.)
Penguin Ireland, 25 St Stephen's Green, Dublin 2, Ireland (a division of Penguin Books Ltd)
Penguin Group (Australia), 250 Camberwell Road, Camberwell, Victoria 3124, Australia
(a division of Pearson Australia Group Pty Ltd)
Penguin Books India Pvt Ltd, 11 Community Centre, Panchsheel Park,
New Delhi – 110 017, India
Penguin Group (NZ), 67 Apollo Drive, Rosedale, North Shore 0632, New Zealand
(a division of Pearson New Zealand Ltd)
Penguin Books (South Africa) (Pty) Ltd, 24 Sturdee Avenue, Rosebank, Johannesburg 2196,
South Africa

Penguin Books Ltd, Registered Offices: 80 Strand, London WC2R ORL, England

www.penguin.com

Selected from *The Ballad of the Sad Café*, published in Penguin Classics 2001
This selection published in Penguin Classics 2011
004

Copyright © Carson McCullers, 1951

Typeset by Jouve (UK), Milton Keynes
Printed in England by Clays Ltd, St Ives plc

ISBN: 978-0-141-19612-1

www.greenpenguin.co.uk

Penguin Books is committed to a sustainable
future for our business, our readers and our planet.
This book is made from Forest Stewardship
Council™ certified paper.

ALWAYS LEARNING   PEARSON

Contents

Wunderkind

She came into the living-room, her music satchel plopping against her winter-stockinged legs and her other arm weighted down with school books, and stood for a moment listening to the sounds from the studio. A soft procession of piano chords and the tuning of a violin. Then Mister Bilderbach called out to her in his chunky, guttural tones:

'That you, Bienchen?'

As she jerked off her mittens she saw that her fingers were twitching to the motions of the fugue she had practised that morning. 'Yes,' she answered. 'It's me.'

'I,' the voice corrected. 'Just a moment.'

She could hear Mister Lafkowitz talking – his words spun out in a silky, unintelligible hum. A voice almost like a woman's, she thought, compared to Mister Bilderbach's. Restlessness scattered her attention. She fumbled with her geometry book and *Le Voyage de Monsieur Perichon* before putting them on the table. She sat down on the sofa and began to take her music from the satchel. Again she saw her hands – the quivering tendons that stretched down from her knuckles, the sore finger-tip capped with curled, dingy tape. The sight sharpened the fear that had begun to torment her for the past few months.

Noiselessly she mumbled a few phrases of encouragement to herself. A good lesson – a good lesson – like it used to be. Her lips closed as she heard the stolid sound of Mister Bilderbach's footsteps across the floor of the studio and the creaking of the door as it slid open.

For a moment she had the peculiar feeling that during most of the fifteen years of her life she had been looking at the face and shoulders that jutted from behind the door, in a silence disturbed only by the muted, blank plucking of a violin string. Mister Bilderbach. Her teacher, Mister Bilderbach. The quick eyes behind the horn-rimmed glasses; the light, thin hair and the narrow face beneath; the lips full and loose shut and the lower one pink and shining from the bites of his teeth; the forked veins in his temples throbbing plainly enough to be observed across the room.

'Aren't you a little early?' he asked, glancing at the clock on the mantelpiece that had pointed to five minutes of twelve for a month. 'Josef's in here. We're running over a little sonatina by someone he knows.'

'Good,' she said, trying to smile. 'I'll listen.' She could see her fingers sinking powerless into a blur of piano keys. She felt tired – felt that if he looked at her much longer her hands might tremble.

He stood uncertain, half-way in the room. Sharply his teeth pushed down on his bright, swollen lip. 'Hungry, Bienchen?' he asked. 'There's some apple cake Anna made, and milk.'

'I'll wait till afterward,' she said. 'Thanks.'

'After you finish with a very fine lesson – eh?' His smile seemed to crumble at the corners.

There was a sound from behind him in the studio and Mister Lafkowitz pushed at the other panel of the door and stood beside him.

'Frances?' he said, smiling. 'And how is the work coming now?'

Without meaning to, Mister Lafkowitz always made her feel clumsy and overgrown. He was such a small man himself, with a weary look when he was not holding his violin. His eyebrows curved high above his sallow, Jewish face as though asking a question, but the lids of his eyes drowsed languorous and indifferent. Today he seemed distracted. She watched him come into the room for no apparent purpose, holding his pearl-tipped bow in his still fingers, slowly gliding the white horsehair through a chalky piece of rosin. His eyes were sharp bright slits today and the linen handkerchief that flowed down from his collar darkened the shadows beneath them.

'I gather you're doing a lot now,' smiled Mister Lafkowitz, although she had not yet answered the question.

She looked at Mister Bilderbach. He turned away. His heavy shoulders pushed the door open wide so that the late afternoon sun came through the window of the studio and shafted yellow over the dusty living-room. Behind her teacher she could see the squat long piano, the window, and the bust of Brahms.

'No,' she said to Mister Lafkowitz, 'I'm doing terribly.' Her thin fingers flipped at the pages of her music. 'I don't know what's the matter,' she said, looking at Mister Bilderbach's stooped muscular back that stood tense and listening.

Mister Lafkowitz smiled. 'There are times, I suppose, when one –'

A harsh chord sounded from the piano. 'Don't you think we'd better get on with this?' asked Mister Bilderbach.

'Immediately,' said Mister Lafkowitz, giving the bow one more scrape before starting towards the door. She could see him pick up his violin from the top of the piano. He caught her eye and lowered the instrument. 'You've seen the picture of Heime?'

Her fingers curled tight over the sharp corner of the satchel. 'What picture?'

'One of Heime in the *Musical Courier* there on the table. Inside the top cover.'

The sonatina began. Discordant yet somehow simple. Empty but with a sharp-cut style of its own. She reached for the magazine and opened it.

There Heime was – in the left-hand corner. Holding his violin with his fingers hooked down over the strings for a pizzicato. With his dark serge knickers strapped neatly beneath his knees, a sweater and rolled collar. It was a bad picture. Although it was snapped in profile his eyes were cut around towards the photographer and his finger looked as though it would pluck the wrong string. He seemed suffering to turn around towards the picture-taking apparatus. He was thinner – his stomach did not poke out now – but he hadn't changed much in six months.

Heime Israelsky, talented young violinist, snapped while at work in his teacher's studio on Riverside Drive. Young Master Israelsky, who will soon celebrate his fifteenth birthday, has been invited to play the Beethoven Concerto with –

That morning, after she had practised from six until eight, her dad had made her sit down at the table with the family for breakfast. She hated breakfast; it gave her a sick feeling afterward. She would rather wait and get four chocolate bars with her twenty cents lunch money and munch them during school – bringing up little morsels from her pocket under cover of her handker- chief, stopping dead when the silver paper rattled. But this morning her dad had put a fried egg on her plate and she had known that if it burst – so that the slimy yellow oozed over the white – she would cry. And that had happened. The same feeling was upon her now. Gingerly she laid the magazine back on the table and closed her eyes.

The music in the studio seemed to be urging vio- lently and clumsily for something that was not to be had. After a moment her thoughts drew back from Heime and the concerto and the picture – and hovered around the lesson once more. She slid over on the sofa until she could see plainly into the studio – the two of them playing, peering at the notations on the piano, lustfully drawing out all that was there.

She could not forget the memory of Mister Bilder- bach's face as he had stared at her a moment ago. Her hands, still twitching unconsciously to the motions of the fugue, closed over her bony knees. Tired, she was.

And with a circling, sinking away feeling like the one that often came to her just before she dropped off to sleep on the nights when she had over-practised. Like those weary half-dreams that buzzed and carried her out into their own whirling space.

A *Wunderkind* – a *Wunderkind* a *Wunderkind*. The syllables would come out rolling in the deep German way, roar against her ears and then fall to a murmur. Along with the faces circling, swelling out in distortion, diminishing to pale blobs – Mister Bilderbach, Mrs Bilderbach, Heime, Mister Lafkowitz. Around and around in a circle revolving to the guttural *Wunderkind*. Mister Bilderbach looming large in the middle of the circle, his face urging – with the others around him.

Phrases of music see-sawing crazily. Notes she had been practising falling over each other like a handful of marbles dropped downstairs. Bach, Debussy, Prokofiev, Brahms – timed grotesquely to the far-off throb of her tired body and the buzzing circle.

Sometimes – when she had not worked more than three hours or had stayed out from high school – the dreams were not so confused. The music soared clearly in her mind and quick, precise little memories would come back – clear as the sissy 'Age of Innocence' picture Heime had given her after their joint concert was over.

A *Wunderkind* – a *Wunderkind*. That was what Mister

Bilderbach had called her when, at twelve, she first came to him. Older pupils had repeated the word.

Not that he had ever said the word to her. 'Bienchen –' (She had a plain American name but he never used it except when her mistakes were enormous.) 'Bienchen,' he would say, 'I know it must be terrible. Carrying around all the time a head that thick. Poor Bienchen –'

Mister Bilderbach's father had been a Dutch violinist. His mother was from Prague. He had been born in this country and had spent his youth in Germany. So many times she wished she had not been born and brought up in just Cincinnati. How do you say *cheese* in German? Mister Bilderbach, what is Dutch for *I don't understand you*?

The first day she came to the studio. After she played the whole Second Hungarian Rhapsody from memory. The room greying with twilight. His face as he leaned over the piano.

'Now we begin all over,' he said that first day. 'It – playing music – is more than cleverness. If a twelve-year-old girl's fingers cover so many keys to a second – that means nothing.'

He tapped his broad chest and his forehead with his stubby hand. 'Here and here. You are old enough to understand that.' He lighted a cigarette and gently blew the first exhalation above her head. 'And work –

work – work – We will start now with these Bach Inventions and these little Schumann pieces.' His hands moved again – this time to jerk the cord of the lamp behind her and point to the music. 'I will show you how I wish this practised. Listen carefully now.'

She had been at the piano for almost three hours and was very tired. His deep voice sounded as though it had been straying inside her for a long time. She wanted to reach out and touch his muscle-flexed finger that pointed out the phrases, wanted to feel the gleaming gold band ring and the strong hairy back of his hand.

She had lessons Tuesday after school and on Saturday afternoons. Often she stayed, when the Saturday lesson was finished, for dinner, and then spent the night and took the streetcar home the next morning. Mrs Bilderbach liked her in her calm, almost dumb way. She was much different from her husband. She was quiet and fat and slow. When she wasn't in the kitchen, cooking the rich dishes that both of them loved, she seemed to spend all her time in their bed upstairs, reading magazines or just looking with a half-smile at nothing. When they had married in Germany she had been a *Lieder* singer. She didn't sing any more (she said it was her throat). When he would call her in from the kitchen to listen to a pupil she would always smile and say that it was *gut*, very *gut*.

When Frances was thirteen it came to her one day that the Bilderbachs had no children. It seemed strange. Once she had been back in the kitchen with Mrs Bilderbach when he had come striding in from the studio, tense with anger at some pupil who had annoyed him. His wife stood stirring the thick soup until his hand groped out and rested on her shoulder. Then she turned – stood placid – while he folded his arms about her and buried his sharp face in the white, nerveless flesh of her neck. They stood that way without moving. And then his face jerked back suddenly, the anger diminished to a quiet inexpressiveness, and he had returned to the studio.

After she had started with Mister Bilderbach and didn't have time to see anything of the people at high school, Heime had been the only friend of her own age. He was Mister Lafkowitz's pupil and would come with him to Mister Bilderbach's on evenings when she would be there. They would listen to their teachers' playing. And often they themselves went over chamber music together – Mozart sonatas or Bloch.

A *Wunderkind* – a *Wunderkind*.

Heime was a *Wunderkind*. He and she, then.

Heime had been playing the violin since he was four. He didn't have to go to school; Mister Lafkowitz's brother, who was crippled, used to teach him geometry and European history and French verbs in the afternoon. When he was thirteen he had as fine a technique as any violinist in Cincinnati – everyone said so. But playing the violin must be easier than the piano. She knew it must be.

Heime always seemed to smell of corduroy pants and the food he had eaten and rosin. Half the time, too, his hands were dirty around the knuckles and the cuffs of his shirts peeped out dingily from the sleeves of his sweater. She always watched his hands when he played – thin only at the joints with the hard little blobs of flesh bulging over the short-cut nails and the babyish-looking crease that showed so plainly in his bowing wrist.

In the dreams, as when she was awake, she could remember the concert only in a blur. She had not known it was unsuccessful for her until months after. True, the papers had praised Heime more than her. But he was much shorter than she. When they stood together on the stage he came only to her shoulders. And that made a difference with people, she knew. Also, there was the matter of the sonata they played together. The Bloch.

'No, no – I don't think that would be appropriate,' Mister Bilderbach had said when the Bloch was suggested to end the programme. 'Now that John Powell thing – the Sonate Virginianesque.'

She hadn't understood then; she wanted it to be the Bloch as much as Mister Lafkowitz and Heime.

Mister Bilderbach had given in. Later, after the reviews had said she lacked the temperament for that type of music, after they called her playing thin and lacking in feeling, she felt cheated.

'That oie oie stuff,' said Mister Bilderbach, crackling the newspapers at her. 'Not for you, Bienchen. Leave all that to the Heimes and vitses and skys.'

A *Wunderkind*. No matter what the papers said, that was what he had called her.

Why was it Heime had done so much better at the concert than she? At school sometimes, when she was supposed to be watching someone do a geometry problem on the blackboard, the question would twist knife-like inside her. She would worry about it in bed, and even sometimes when she was supposed to be concentrating at the piano. It wasn't just the Bloch and her not being Jewish – not entirely. It wasn't that Heime didn't have to go to school and had begun his training so early, either. It was – ?

Once she thought she knew.

'Play the Fantasia and Fugue,' Mister Bilderbach had demanded one evening a year ago – after he and Mister Lafkowitz had finished reading some music together.

The Bach, as she played, seemed to her well done. From the tail of her eyes she could see the calm, pleased expression on Mister Bilderbach's face, see his hands rise climactically from the chair arms and then sink down loose and satisfied when the high points of the phrases had been passed successfully. She stood up from the piano when it was over, swallowing to loosen the bands that the music seemed to have drawn around her throat and chest. But –

'Frances –' Mister Lafkowitz had said then, suddenly, looking at her with his thin mouth curved and his eyes almost covered by their delicate lids. 'Do you know how many children Bach had?'

She turned to him, puzzled. 'A good many. Twenty some odd.'

'Well then –' The corners of his smile etched themselves gently in his pale face. 'He could not have been so cold – then.'

Mister Bilderbach was not pleased; his guttural effulgence of German words had *Kind* in it somewhere. Mister Lafkowitz raised his eyebrows. She had caught the point easily enough, but she felt no deception in keeping her face blank and immature because that was the way Mister Bilderbach wanted her to look.

Yet such things had nothing to do with it. Nothing very much, at least, for she would grow older. Mister Bilderbach understood that, and even Mister Lafkowitz had not meant just what he said.

In the dreams Mister Bilderbach's face loomed out

and contracted in the centre of the whirling circle. The lips surging softly, the veins in his temples insisting.

But sometimes, before she slept, there were such clear memories; as when she pulled a hole in the heel of her stocking down, so that her shoe would hide it. 'Bienchen, Bienchen!' And bringing Mrs Bilderbach's work-basket in and showing her how it should be darned and not gathered together in a lumpy heap.

And the time she graduated from Junior High.

'What you wear?' asked Mrs Bilderbach the Sunday morning at breakfast when she told them about how they had practised to march into the auditorium.

'An evening dress my cousin had last year.'

'Ah – Bienchen!' he said, circling his warm coffee cup with his heavy hands, looking up at her with wrinkles around his laughing eyes. 'I bet I know what Bienchen wants –'

He insisted. He would not believe her when she explained that she honestly didn't care at all.

'Like this, Anna,' he said, pushing his napkin across the table and mincing to the other side of the room, swishing his hips, rolling up his eyes behind his horn-rimmed glasses.

The next Saturday afternoon, after her lessons, he took her to the department stores downtown. His thick fingers smoothed over the filmy nets and crackling taffetas that the saleswomen unwound from their bolts. He held colours to her face, cocking his head to one side, and selected pink. Shoes, he remembered too. He liked best some white kid pumps. They seemed a little like old ladies' shoes to her and the Red Cross in the instep had a charity look. But it really didn't matter at all. When Mrs Bilderbach began to cut out the dress and fit it to her with pins, he interrupted his lessons to stand by and suggest ruffles around the hips and neck and a fancy rosette on the shoulder. The music was coming along nicely then. Dresses and commencement and such made no difference.

Nothing mattered much except playing the music as it must be played, bringing out the thing that must be in her, practising, practising, playing so that Mister Bilderbach's face lost some of its urging look. Putting the thing into her music that Myra Hess had, and Yehudi Menuhin – even Heime!

What had begun to happen to her four months ago? The notes began springing out with a glib, dead intonation. Adolescence, she thought. Some kids played with promise – and worked and worked until, like her, the least little thing would start them crying, and worn out with trying to get the thing across – the longing thing they felt – something queer began to happen –. But not she! She was like Heime. She had to be. She –

Once it was there for sure. And you didn't lose things like that. A *Wunderkind* . . . A *Wunderkind* . . . Of her he said it, rolling the words in the sure, deep German way. And in the dreams even deeper, more certain than ever. With his face looming out at her, and the longing phrases of music mixed in with the zooming, circling round, round, round – A *Wunderkind*. A *Wunderkind* . . .

This afternoon Mister Bilderbach did not show Mister Lafkowitz to the front door, as he usually did. He stayed at the piano, softly pressing a solitary note. Listening, Frances watched the violinist wind his scarf about his pale throat.

'A good picture of Heime,' she said, picking up her music. 'I got a letter from him a couple of months ago – telling about hearing Schnabel and Huberman and about Carnegie Hall and things to eat at the Russian Tea Room.'

To put off going into the studio a moment longer she waited until Mister Lafkowitz was ready to leave and then stood behind him as he opened the door. The frosty cold outside cut into the room. It was growing late and the air was seeped with the pale yellow of winter twilight. When the door swung to on its hinges, the house seemed darker and more silent than ever before she had known it to be.

As she went into the studio Mister Bilderbach got up

from the piano and silently watched her settle herself at the keyboard.

'Well, Bienchen,' he said, 'this afternoon we are going to begin all over. Start from scratch. Forget the last few months.'

He looked as though he were trying to act a part in a movie. His solid body swayed from toe to heel, he rubbed his hands together, and even smiled in a satisfied, movie way. Then suddenly he thrust this manner brusquely aside. His heavy shoulders slouched and he began to run through the stack of music she had brought in. 'The Bach – no, not yet,' he murmured. 'The Beethoven? Yes, the Variation Sonata. Opus 26.'

The keys of the piano hemmed her in – stiff and white and dead-seeming.

'Wait a minute,' he said. He stood in the curve of the piano, elbows propped, and looked at her. 'Today I expect something from you. Now this sonata – it's the first Beethoven sonata you ever worked on. Every note is under control – technically – you have nothing to cope with but the music. Only music now. That's all you think about.'

He rustled through the pages of her volume until he found the place. Then he pulled his teaching chair halfway across the room, turned it around and seated himself, straddling the back with his legs.

For some reason, she knew, this position of his usually had a good effect on her performance. But today she felt that she would notice him from the corner of her eye and be disturbed. His back was stiffly tilted, his legs looked tense. The heavy volume before him seemed to balance dangerously on the chair back. 'Now we begin,' he said with a peremptory dart of his eyes in her direction.

Her hands rounded over the keys and then sank down. The first notes were too loud, the other phrases followed dryly.

Arrestingly his hand rose up from the score. 'Wait! Think a minute what you're playing. How is this beginning marked?'

'*An-andante.*'

'All right. Don't drag it into an *adagio* then. And play deeply into the keys. Don't snatch it off shallowly that way. A graceful, deep-toned *andante* –'

She tried again. Her hands seemed separate from the music that was in her.

'Listen,' he interrupted. 'Which of these variations dominates the whole?'

'The dirge,' she answered.

'Then prepare for that. This is an *andante* – but it's not salon stuff as you just played it. Start out softly, *piano*, and make it swell out just before the *arpeggio*.

Make it warm and dramatic. And down here – where it's marked *dolce* make the counter-melody sing out. You know all that. We've gone over all that side of it before. Now play it. Feel it as Beethoven wrote it down. Feel that tragedy and restraint.'

She could not stop looking at his hands. They seemed to rest tentatively on the music, ready to fly up as a stop signal as soon as she would begin, the gleaming flash of his ring calling her to halt. 'Mister Bilderbach – maybe if I – if you let me play on through the first variation without stopping I could do better.'

'I won't interrupt,' he said.

Her pale face leaned over too close to the keys. She played through the first part, and, obeying a nod from him, began the second. There were no flaws that jarred on her, but the phrases shaped from her fingers before she had put into them the meaning that she felt.

When she had finished he looked up from the music and began to speak with dull bluntness: 'I hardly heard those harmonic fillings in the right hand. And, incidentally, this part was supposed to take on intensity, develop the foreshadowings that were supposed to be inherent in the first part. Go on with the next one, though.'

She wanted to start it with subdued viciousness and progress to a feeling of deep, swollen sorrow. Her mind told her that. But her hands seemed to gum in the keys like limp macaroni and she could not imagine the music as it should be.

When the last note had stopped vibrating, he closed the book and deliberately got up from the chair. He was moving his lower jaw from side to side – and between his open lips she could glimpse the pink healthy lane to his throat and his strong, smoke-yellowed teeth. He laid the Beethoven gingerly on top of the rest of her music and propped his elbows on the smooth, black piano top once more. 'No,' he said simply, looking at her.

Her mouth began to quiver. 'I can't help it. I –'

Suddenly he strained his lips into a smile. 'Listen, Bienchen,' he began in a new, forced voice. 'You still play the "Harmonious Blacksmith", don't you? I told you not to drop it from your repertoire.'

'Yes,' she said. 'I practise it now and then.'

His voice was the one he used for children. 'It was among the first things we worked on together – remember. So strongly you used to play it – like a real blacksmith's daughter. You see, Bienchen, I know you so well – as if you were my own girl. I know what you have – I've heard you play so many things beautifully. You used to –'

He stopped in confusion and inhaled from his pulpy stub of cigarette. The smoke drowsed out from his pink lips and clung in a grey mist around her lank hair and childish forehead.

'Make it happy and simple,' he said, switching on the lamp behind her and stepping back from the piano.

For a moment he stood just inside the bright circle the light made. Then impulsively he squatted down to the floor. 'Vigorous,' he said.

She could not stop looking at him, sitting on one heel with the other foot resting squarely before him for balance, the muscles of his strong thighs straining under the cloth of his trousers, his back straight, his elbows staunchly propped on his knees. 'Simply now,' he repeated with a gesture of his fleshy hands. 'Think of the blacksmith – working out in the sunshine all day. Working easily and undisturbed.'

She could not look down at the piano. The light brightened the hairs on the backs of his outspread hands, made the lenses of his glasses glitter.

'All of it,' he urged. 'Now!'

She felt that the marrows of her bones were hollow and there was no blood left in her. Her heart that had been springing against her chest all afternoon felt suddenly dead. She saw it grey and limp and shrivelled at the edges like an oyster.

His face seemed to throb out in space before her,

come closer with the lurching motion in the veins of his temples. In retreat, she looked down at the piano. Her lips shook like jelly and a surge of noiseless tears made the white keys blur in a watery line. 'I can't,' she whispered. 'I don't know why, but I just can't – can't any more.'

His tense body slackened and, holding his hand to his side, he pulled himself up. She clutched her music and hurried past him.

Her coat. The mittens and galoshes. The schoolbooks and the satchel he had given her on her birthday. All from the silent room that was hers. Quickly – before he would have to speak.

As she passed through the vestibule she could not help but see his hands – held out from his body that leaned against the studio door, relaxed and purposeless. The door shut to firmly. Dragging her books and satchel she stumbled down the stone steps, turned in the wrong direction, and hurried down the street that had become confused with noise and bicycles and the games of other children.

The Jockey

The jockey came to the doorway of the dining-room, then after a moment stepped to one side and stood motionless, with his back to the wall. The room was crowded, as this was the third day of the season and all the hotels in the town were full. In the dining-room bouquets of August roses scattered their petals on the white table linen and from the adjoining bar came a warm, drunken wash of voices. The jockey waited with his back to the wall and scrutinized the room with pinched, crêpy eyes. He examined the room until at last his eyes reached a table in a corner diagonally across from him, at which three men were sitting. As he watched, the jockey raised his chin and tilted his head back to one side, his dwarfed body grew rigid, and his hands stiffened so that the fingers curled inward like grey claws. Tense against the wall of the dining-room, he watched and waited in this way.

He was wearing a suit of green Chinese silk that

evening, tailored precisely and the size of a costume outfit for a child. The shirt was yellow, the tie striped with pastel colours. He had no hat with him and wore his hair brushed down in a stiff, wet bang on his forehead. His face was drawn, ageless, and grey. There were shadowed hollows at his temples and his mouth was set in a wiry smile. After a time he was aware that he had been seen by one of the three men he had been watching. But the jockey did not nod; he only raised his chin still higher and hooked the thumb of his tense hand in the pocket of his coat.

The three men at the corner table were a trainer, a bookie, and a rich man. The trainer was Sylvester – a large, loosely built fellow with a flushed nose and slow blue eyes. The bookie was Simmons. The rich man was the owner of a horse named Seltzer, which the jockey had ridden that afternoon. The three of them drank whisky with soda, and a whit-coated waiter had just brought on the main course of the dinner.

It was Sylvester who first saw the jockey. He looked away quickly, put down his whisky glass, and nervously mashed the tip of his red nose with his thumb. 'It's Bitsy Barlow,' he said. 'Standing over there across the room. Just watching us.'

'Oh, the jockey,' said the rich man. He was facing the

wall and he half turned his head to look behind him. 'Ask him over.'

'God no,' Sylvester said.

'He's crazy,' Simmons said. The bookie's voice was flat and without inflexion. He had the face of a born gambler, carefully adjusted, the expression a permanent deadlock between fear and greed.

'Well, I wouldn't call him that exactly,' said Sylvester. 'I've known him a long time. He was O.K. until about six months ago. But if he goes on like this, I can't see him lasting another year. I just can't.'

'It was what happened in Miami,' said Simmons.

'What?' asked the rich man.

Sylvester glanced across the room at the jockey and wet the corner of his mouth with his red, fleshy tongue. 'An accident. A kid got hurt on the track. Broke a leg and a hip. He was a particular pal of Bitsy's. An Irish kid. Not a bad rider, either.'

'That's a pity,' said the rich man.

'Yeah. They were particular friends,' Sylvester said. 'You would always find him up in Bitsy's hotel room. They would be playing rummy or else lying on the floor reading the sports page together.'

'Well, those things happen,' said the rich man.

Simmons cut into his beefsteak. He held his fork

prongs downward on the plate and carefully piled on mushrooms with the blade of his knife. 'He's crazy,' he repeated. 'He gives me the creeps.'

All the tables in the dining-room were occupied. There was a party at the banquet table in the centre, and green white August moths had found their way in from the night and fluttered about the clear candle flames. Two girls wearing flannel slacks and blazers walked arm in arm across the room into the bar. From the main street outside came the echoes of holiday hysteria.

'They claim that in August Saratoga is the wealthiest town per capita in the world.' Sylvester turned to the rich man. 'What do you think?'

'I wouldn't know,' said the rich man. 'It may very well be so.'

Daintily, Simmons wiped his greasy mouth with the tip of his forefinger. 'How about Hollywood? And Wall Street –'

'Wait,' said Sylvester. 'He's decided to come over here.'

The jockey had left the wall and was approaching the table in the corner. He walked with a prim strut, swinging out his legs in a half-circle with each step, his heels biting smartly into the red velvet carpet on the floor. On the way over he brushed against the elbow of a fat woman in white satin at the banquet table; he stepped back and bowed with dandified courtesy, his eyes quite closed. When he had crossed the room he drew up a chair and sat at a corner of the table, between Sylvester and the rich man, without a nod of greeting or a change in his set, grey face.

'Had dinner?' Sylvester asked.

'Some people might call it that.' The jockey's voice was high, bitter, clear.

Sylvester put his knife and fork down carefully on his plate. The rich man shifted his position, turning sidewise in his chair and crossing his legs. He was dressed in twill riding pants, unpolished boots, and a shabby brown jacket – this was his outfit day and night in the racing season, although he was never seen on a horse. Simmons went on with his dinner.

'Like a spot of seltzer water?' asked Sylvester. 'Or something like that?'

The jockey didn't answer. He drew a gold cigarette case from his pocket and snapped it open. Inside were a few cigarettes and a tiny gold penknife. He used the knife to cut a cigarette in half. When he had lighted his smoke he held up his hand to a waiter passing by the table. 'Kentucky bourbon, please.'

'Now listen, Kid,' said Sylvester.

'Don't Kid me.'

'Be reasonable. You know you got to behave reasonable.'

The jockey drew up the left corner of his mouth in a stiff jeer. His eyes lowered to the food spread out on the table, but instantly he looked up again. Before the rich man was a fish casserole, baked in a cream sauce and garnished with parsley. Sylvester had ordered eggs Benedict. There was asparagus, fresh buttered corn, and a side dish of wet black olives. A plate of French-fried potatoes was in the corner of the table before the jockey. He didn't look at the food again, but kept his pinched eyes on the centre-piece of full-blown lavender roses. 'I don't suppose you remember a certain person by the name of McGuire,' he said.

'Now, listen,' said Sylvester.

The waiter brought the whisky, and the jockey sat fondling the glass with his small, strong, callused hands. On his wrist was a gold link bracelet that clinked against the table edge. After turning the glass between his palms, the jockey suddenly drank the whisky neat in two hard swallows. He set down the glass sharply. 'No, I don't suppose your memory is that long and extensive,' he said.

'Sure enough, Bitsy,' said Sylvester. 'What makes you act like this? You hear from the kid today?'

'I received a letter,' the jockey said. 'The certain person we were speaking about was taken out from the cast on Wednesday. One leg is two inches shorter than the other. That's all.'

Sylvester clucked his tongue and shook his head. 'I realize how you feel.'

'Do you?' The jockey was looking at the dishes on the table. His gaze passed from the fish casserole to the corn, and finally fixed on the plate of fried potatoes. His face tightened and quickly he looked up again. A rose shattered and he picked up one of the petals, bruised it between his thumb and forefinger, and put it in his mouth.

'Well, those things happen,' said the rich man.

The trainer and the bookie had finished eating, but there was food left on the serving dishes before their plates. The rich man dipped his buttery fingers in his water glass and wiped them with his napkin.

'Well,' said the jockey. 'Doesn't somebody want me to pass them something? Or maybe perhaps you desire to re-order. Another hunk of beefsteak, gentle-men, or –'

'Please,' said Sylvester. 'Be reasonable. Why don't you go on upstairs?'

'Yes, why don't I?' the jockey said.

His prim voice had risen higher and there was about it the sharp whine of hysteria.

'Why don't I go up to my goddamn room and walk around and write some letters and go to bed like a good boy? Why don't I just –' He pushed his chair back and got up. 'Oh, foo,' he said. 'Foo to you. I want a drink.'

'All I can say is it's your funeral,' said Sylvester. 'You know what it does to you. You know well enough.'

The jockey crossed the dining-room and went into the bar. He ordered a Manhattan, and Sylvester watched him stand with his heels pressed tight together, his body hard as a lead soldier's, holding his little finger out from the cocktail glass and sipping the drink slowly.

'He's crazy,' said Simmons. 'Like I said.'

Sylvester turned to the rich man. 'If he eats a lamb chop, you can see the shape of it in his stomach an hour afterwards. He can't sweat things out of him any more. He's a hundred and twelve and a half. He's gained three pounds since we left Miami.'

'A jockey shouldn't drink,' said the rich man.

'The food don't satisfy him like it used to and he can't sweat it out. If he eats a lamb chop, you can watch it tooching out in his stomach and it don't go down.'

The jockey finished his Manhattan. He swallowed, crushed the cherry in the bottom of the glass with his thumb, then pushed the glass away from him. The two girls in blazers were standing at his left, their faces turned towards each other, and at the other end of the bar two touts had started an argument about which was the highest mountain in the world. Everyone was with somebody else; there was no other person drinking alone that night. The jockey paid with a brand-new fifty-dollar bill and didn't count the change.

He walked back to the dining-room and to the table at which the three men were sitting, but he did not sit down. 'No, I wouldn't presume to think your memory is that extensive,' he said. He was so small that the edge of the table-top reached almost to his belt, and when he gripped the corner with his wiry hands he didn't have to stoop. 'No, you're too busy gobbling up dinners in dining-rooms. You're too –'

'Honestly,' begged Sylvester. 'You got to behave reasonable.'

'Reasonable! Reasonable!' The jockey's grey face quivered, then set in a mean, frozen grin. He shook the table so that the plates rattled, and for a moment it seemed that he would push it over. But suddenly he stopped. His hand reached out towards the plate nearest to him and deliberately he put a few of the French-fried potatoes in his mouth. He chewed slowly, his upper lip raised, then he turned and spat out the pulpy mouthful on the smooth red carpet which covered the floor. 'Libertines,' he said, and his voice was thin and broken. He rolled the word in his mouth, as though it had a flavour and a substance that gratified him. 'You libertines,' he said again, and turned and walked with his rigid swagger out of the dining-room.

Sylvester shrugged one of his loose, heavy shoulders. The rich man sopped up some water that had been spilled on the tablecloth, and they didn't speak until the waiter came to clear away.

Madame Zilensky and the King of Finland

To Mr Brook, the head of the music department at Ryder College, was due all the credit for getting Madame Zilensky on the faculty. The college considered itself fortunate; her reputation was impressive, both as a composer and as a pedagogue. Mr Brook took on himself the responsibility of finding a house for Madame Zilensky, a comfortable place with a garden, which was convenient to the college and next to the apartment house where he himself lived.

No one in Westbridge had known Madame Zilensky before she came. Mr Brook had seen her pictures in musical journals, and once he had written to her about the authenticity of a certain Buxtehude manuscript. Also, when it was being settled that she was to join the faculty, they had exchanged a few cables and letters on practical affairs. She wrote in a clear, square hand, and

the only thing out of the ordinary in these letters was
the fact that they contained an occasional reference to
objects and persons altogether unknown to Mr Brook,
such as 'the yellow cat in Lisbon' or 'poor Heinrich'.
These lapses Mr Brook put down to the confusion of
getting herself and her family out of Europe.

Mr Brook was a somewhat pastel person; years of
Mozart minuets, of explanations about diminished sev-
enths and minor triads, had given him a watchful
vocational patience. For the most part, he kept to himself. He loathed academic fiddle-faddle and committees.
Years before, when the music department had decided
to gang together and spend the summer in Salzburg,
Mr Brook sneaked out of the arrangement at the last
moment and took a solitary trip to Peru. He had a few
eccentricities himself and was tolerant of the peculiari-
ties of others; indeed, he rather relished the ridiculous.
Often, when confronted with some grave and incon-
gruous situation, he would feel a little inside tickle,
which stiffened his long, mild face and sharpened the
light in his grey eyes.

Mr Brook met Madame Zilensky at the Westbridge
station a week before the beginning of the fall semester.
He recognized her instantly. She was a tall, straight
woman with a pale and haggard face. Her eyes were
deeply shadowed and she wore her dark, ragged hair

pushed back from her forehead. She had large, delicate hands, which were very grubby. About her person as a whole there was something noble and abstract that made Mr Brook draw back for a moment and stand nervously undoing his cuff-links. In spite of her clothes – a long, black skirt and a broken-down old leather jacket – she made an impression of vague elegance. With Madame Zilensky were three children, boys between the ages of ten and six, all blond, blank-eyed, and beautiful. There was one other person, an old woman who turned out later to be the Finnish servant.

This was the group he found at the station. The only luggage they had with them was two immense boxes of manuscripts, the rest of their paraphernalia having been forgotten in the station at Springfield when they changed trains. This is the sort of thing that can happen to anyone. When Mr Brook got them all into a taxi, he thought the worst difficulties were over, but Madame Zilensky suddenly tried to scramble over his knees and get out of the door.

'My God!' she said. 'I left my – how do you say? – my tick-tick-tick –'

'Your watch?' asked Mr Brook.

'Oh, no!' she said vehemently. 'You know, my tick-tick-tick,' and she waved her forefinger from side to side, pendulum fashion.

'Tick-tick,' said Mr Brook, putting his hands to his forehead and closing his eyes. 'Could you possibly mean a metronome?'

'Yes! Yes! I think I must have lost it there where we changed trains.'

Mr Brook managed to quiet her. He even said, with a kind of dazed gallantry, that he would get her another one the next day. But at the time he was bound to admit to himself that there was something curious about this panic over a metronome when there was all the rest of the lost luggage to consider.

The Zilensky ménage moved into the house next door, and on the surface everything was all right. The boys were quiet children. Their names were Sigmund, Boris, and Sammy. They were always together and they followed each other around Indian file, Sigmund usually the first. Among themselves they spoke a desperate-sounding family Esperanto made up of Russian, French, Finnish, German, and English; when other people were around, they were strangely silent. It was not any one thing that the Zilenskys did or said that made Mr Brook uneasy. There were just little incidents. For example, something about the Zilensky children subconsciously bothered him when they were in a house, and finally he realized that what troubled him was the fact that the

Zilensky boys never walked on a rug; they skirted it single file on the bare floor, and if the room was carpeted, they stood in the doorway and did not go inside. Another thing was this: weeks passed and Madame Zilensky seemed to make no effort to get settled or to furnish the house with anything more than a table and some beds. The front door was left open day and night, and soon the house began to take on a queer, bleak look like that of a place abandoned for years.

The college had every reason to be satisfied with Madame Zilensky. She taught with a fierce insistence. She could become deeply indignant if some Mary Owens or Bernadine Smith would not clean up her Scarlatti trills. She got hold of four pianos for her college studio and set four dazed students to playing Bach fugues together. The racket that came from her end of the department was extraordinary, but Madame Zilensky did not seem to have a nerve in her, and if pure will and effort can get over a musical idea, then Ryder College could not have done better. At night Madame Zilensky worked on her twelfth symphony. She seemed never to sleep; no matter what time of night Mr Brook happened to look out of his sitting-room window, the light in her studio was always on. No, it was not because of any professional consideration that Mr Brook became so dubious.

It was in late October when he felt for the first time that something was unmistakably wrong. He had lunched with Madame Zilensky and had enjoyed himself, as she had given him a very detailed account of an African safari she had made in 1928. Later in the afternoon she stopped in at his office and stood rather abstractly in the doorway.

Mr Brook looked up from his desk and asked, 'Is there anything you want?'

'No, thank you,' said Madame Zilensky. She had a low, beautiful, sombre voice. 'I was only just wondering. You recall the metronome. Do you think perhaps that I might have left it with that French?'

'Who?' asked Mr Brook.

'Why, that French I was married to,' she answered.

'Frenchman,' Mr Brook said mildly. He tried to imagine the husband of Madame Zilensky, but his mind refused. He muttered half to himself, 'The father of the children.'

'But no,' said Madame Zilensky with decision. 'The father of Sammy.'

Mr Brook had a swift prescience. His deepest instincts warned him to say nothing further. Still, his respect for order, his conscience, demanded that he ask, 'And the father of the other two?'

Madame Zilensky put her hand to the back of her head and ruffled up her short, cropped hair. Her face was dreamy, and for several moments she did not answer. Then she said gently, 'Boris is of a Pole who played the piccolo.'

'And Sigmund?' he asked. Mr Brook looked over his orderly desk, with the stack of corrected papers, the three sharpened pencils, the ivory-elephant paper-weight. When he glanced up at Madame Zilensky, she was obviously thinking hard. She gazed around at the corners of the room, her brows lowered and her jaw moving from side to side. At last she said, 'We were discussing the father of Sigmund?'

'Why, no,' said Mr Brook. 'There is no need to do that.'

Madame Zilensky answered in a voice both dignified and final. 'He was a fellow-countryman.'

Mr Brook really did not care one way or the other. He had no prejudices; people could marry seventeen times and have Chinese children so far as he was concerned. But there was something about this conversation with Madame Zilensky that bothered him. Suddenly he understood. The children didn't look at all like Madame Zilensky, but they looked exactly like each other, and as they all had different fathers, Mr Brook thought the resemblance astonishing.

But Madame Zilensky had finished with the subject. She zipped up her leather jacket and turned away.

'That is exactly where I left it,' she said, with a quick nod. '*Chez* that French.'

Affairs in the music department were running smoothly. Mr Brook did not have any serious embarrassments to deal with, such as the harp teacher last year who had finally eloped with a garage mechanic. There was only this nagging apprehension about Madame Zilensky. He could not make out what was wrong in his relations with her or why his feelings were so mixed. To begin with, she was a great globe-trotter, and her conversations were incongruously seasoned with references to far-fetched places. She would go along for days without opening her mouth, prowling through the corridor with her hands in the pockets of her jacket and her face locked in meditation. Then suddenly she would buttonhole Mr Brook and launch out on a long, volatile monologue, her eyes reckless and bright and her voice warm with eagerness. She would talk about anything or nothing at all. Yet, without exception, there was something queer, in a slanted sort of way, about every episode she ever mentioned. If she spoke of taking Sammy to the barbershop, the impression she created was just as foreign as if she were telling of an afternoon in Baghdad. Mr Brook could not make it out.

The truth came to him very suddenly, and the truth made everything perfectly clear, or at least clarified the situation. Mr Brook had come home early and lighted a fire in the little grate in his sitting-room. He felt comfortable and at peace that evening. He sat before the fire in his stockinged feet, with a volume of William Blake on the table by his side, and he had poured himself a half-glass of apricot brandy. At ten o'clock he was drowsing cosily before the fire, his mind full of cloudy phrases of Mahler and floating half-thoughts. Then all at once, out of this delicate stupor, four words came to his mind: 'The King of Finland.' The words seemed familiar, but for the first moment he could not place them. Then all at once he tracked them down. He had been walking across the campus that afternoon when Madame Zilensky stopped him and began some preposterous rigmarole, to which he had only half listened; he was thinking about the stack of canons turned in by his counterpoint class. Now the words, the inflections of her voice, came back to him with insidious exactitude. Madame Zilensky had started off with the following remark: 'One day, when I was standing in front of a *pâtisserie*, the King of Finland came by in a sled.'

Mr Brook jerked himself up straight in his chair and put down his glass of brandy. The woman was a pathological liar. Almost every word she uttered outside of class was an untruth. If she worked all night, she would go out of her way to tell you she spent the evening at the cinema. If she ate lunch at the Old Tavern, she would be sure to mention that she had lunched with her children at home. The woman was simply a pathological liar, and that accounted for everything.

Mr Brook cracked his knuckles and got up from his chair. His first reaction was one of exasperation. That day after day Madame Zilensky would have the gall to sit there in his office and deluge him with her outrageous falsehoods! Mr Brook was intensely provoked. He walked up and down the room, then he went into his kitchenette and made himself a sardine sandwich.

An hour later, as he sat before the fire, his irritation had changed to a scholarly and thoughtful wonder. What he must do, he told himself, was to regard the whole situation impersonally and look on Madame Zilensky as a doctor looks on a sick patient. Her lies were of the guileless sort. She did not dissimulate with any intention to deceive, and the untruths she told were never used to any possible advantage. That was the maddening thing; there was simply no motive behind it all.

Mr Brook finished off the rest of the brandy. And slowly, when it was almost midnight, a further understanding came to him. The reason for the lies of Madame Zilensky was painful and plain. All her life long Madame Zilensky had worked – at the piano, teaching, and writing those beautiful and immense twelve symphonies. Day and night she had drudged and struggled and thrown her soul into her work, and there was not much of her left over for anything else. Being human, she suffered from this lack and did what she could to make up for it. If she passed the evening bent over a table in the library and later declared that she had spent that time playing cards, it was as though she had managed to do both those things. Through the lies, she lived vicariously. The lies doubled the little of her existence that was left over from work and augmented the little rag-end of her personal life.

Mr Brook looked into the fire, and the face of Madame Zilensky was in his mind – a severe face, with dark, weary eyes and delicately disciplined mouth. He was conscious of a warmth in his chest, and a feeling of pity, protectiveness, and dreadful understanding. For a while he was in a state of lovely confusion.

Later on he brushed his teeth and got into his pyjamas. He must be practical. What did this clear up? That French, the Pole with the piccolo, Baghdad? And the children, Sigmund, Boris, and Sammy – who were they? Were they really her children after all, or had she simply rounded them up from somewhere? Mr Brook polished his spectacles and put them on the table by his bed. He must come to an immediate understanding with her. Otherwise, there would exist in the department a situation which could become most problematical. It was two o'clock. He glanced out of his window and saw that the light in Madame Zilensky's workroom was still on. Mr Brook got into bed, made terrible faces in the dark, and tried to plan what he would say next day.

Mr Brook was in his office by eight o'clock. He sat hunched up behind his desk, ready to trap Madame Zilensky as she passed down the corridor. He did not have to wait long, and as soon as he heard her footsteps he called out her name.

Madame Zilensky stood in the doorway. She looked vague and jaded. 'How are you? I had such a fine night's rest,' she said.

'Pray be seated, if you please,' said Mr Brook. 'I would like a word with you.'

Madame Zilensky put aside her portfolio and leaned back wearily in the armchair across from him. 'Yes?' she asked.

'Yesterday you spoke to me as I was walking across the campus,' he said slowly. 'And if I am not mistaken, I believe you said something about a pastry shop and the King of Finland. Is that correct?'

Madame Zilensky turned her head to one side and stared retrospectively at a corner of the window-sill.

'Something about a pastry shop,' he repeated.

Her tired face brightened. 'But of course,' she said eagerly. 'I told you about the time I was standing in front of this shop and the King of Finland –'

'Madame Zilensky!' Mr Brook cried. 'There *is* no King of Finland.'

Madame Zilensky looked absolutely blank. Then, after an instant, she started off again. 'I was standing in front of Bjarne's *pâtisserie* when I turned away from the cakes and suddenly saw the King of Finland –'

'Madame Zilensky, I just told you that there is no King of Finland.'

'In Helsingfors,' she started off again desperately, and again he let her get as far as the King, and then no farther.

'Finland is a democracy,' he said. 'You could not possibly have seen the King of Finland. Therefore, what you have just said is an untruth. A pure untruth.'

Never afterwards could Mr Brook forget the face of Madame Zilensky at that moment. In her eyes there was astonishment, dismay, and a sort of cornered horror. She had the look of one who watches his whole interior world split open and disintegrate.

'It is a pity,' said Mr Brook with real sympathy.

But Madame Zilensky pulled herself together. She raised her chin and said coldly, 'I am a Finn.'

'That I do not question,' answered Mr Brook. On second thought, he did question it a little.

'I was born in Finland and I am a Finnish citizen.'

'That may very well be,' said Mr Brook in a rising voice.

'In the war,' she continued passionately, 'I rode a motor-cycle and was a messenger.'

'Your patriotism does not enter into it.'

'Just because I am getting out the first papers –'

'Madame Zilensky!' said Mr Brook. His hands grasped the edge of the desk. 'That is only an irrelevant issue. The point is that you maintained and testified that you saw – that you saw –' But he could not finish. Her face stopped him. She was deadly pale and there were shadows around her mouth. Her eyes were wide open, doomed, and proud. And Mr Brook felt suddenly like a murderer. A great commotion of feelings – understanding, remorse, and unreasonable love – made him cover his face with his hands. He could not speak until this agitation in his insides quietened down, and then he said very faintly, 'Yes. Of course. The King of Finland. And was he nice?'

An hour later, Mr Brook sat looking out of the window of his office. The trees along the quiet Westbridge street were almost bare, and the grey buildings of the college had a calm, sad look. As he idly took in the familiar scene, he noticed the Drakes' old Airedale waddling along down the street. It was a thing he had watched a hundred times before, so what was it that struck him as strange? Then he realized with a kind of cold surprise that the old dog was running along backwards. Mr Brook watched the Airedale until he was out of sight, then resumed his work on the canons which had been turned in by the class in counterpoint.

A Tree, a Rock, a Cloud

It was raining that morning, and still very dark. When the boy reached the streetcar café he had almost finished his route and he went in for a cup of coffee. The place was an all-night café owned by a bitter and stingy man called Leo. After the raw, empty street the café seemed friendly and bright: along the counter there were a couple of soldiers, three spinners from the cotton-mill, and in a corner a man who sat hunched over with his nose and half his face down in a beer mug. The boy wore a helmet such as aviators wear. When he went into the café he unbuckled the chin-strap and raised the right flap up over his pink little ear; often as he drank his coffee someone would speak to him in a friendly way. But this morning Leo did not look into his face and none of the men were talking. He paid and was leaving the café when a voice called out to him:

'Son! Hey Son!'

He turned back and the man in the corner was

crooking his finger and nodding to him. He had brought his face out of the beer mug and he seemed suddenly very happy. The man was long and pale, with a big nose and faded orange hair.

'Hey, Son!'

The boy went towards him. He was an undersized boy of about twelve, with one shoulder drawn higher than the other because of the weight of the paper-sack. His face was shallow, freckled, and his eyes were round child eyes.

'Yeah, Mister?'

The man laid one hand on the paper-boy's shoulders, then grasped the boy's chin and turned his face slowly from one side to the other. The boy shrank back uneasily.

'Say! What's the big idea?'

The boy's voice was shrill; inside the café it was suddenly very quiet.

The man said slowly: 'I love you.'

All along the counter the men laughed. The boy, who had scowled and sidled away, did not know what to do. He looked over the counter at Leo, and Leo watched him with a weary, brittle jeer. The boy tried to laugh also. But the man was serious and sad.

'I did not mean to tease you, Son,' he said. 'Sit down and have a beer with me. There is something I have to explain.'

Cautiously, out of the corner of his eye, the paper-boy questioned the men along the counter to see what he should do. But they had gone back to their beer or their breakfast and did not notice him. Leo put a cup of coffee on the counter and a little jug of cream.

'He is a minor,' Leo said.

The paper-boy slid himself up on to the stool. His ear beneath the upturned flap of the helmet was very small and red. The man was nodding at him soberly. 'It is important,' he said. Then he reached in his hip pocket and brought out something which he held up in the palm of his hand for the boy to see.

'Look very carefully,' he said.

The boy stared, but there was nothing to look at very carefully. The man held in his big, grimy palm a photograph. It was the face of a woman, but blurred, so that only the hat and the dress she was wearing stood out clearly.

'See?' the man asked.

The boy nodded and the man placed another picture in his palm. The woman was standing on a beach in a bathing suit. The suit made her stomach very big, and that was the main thing you noticed.

'Got a good look?' He leaned over closer and finally asked: 'You ever seen her before?'

The boy sat motionless, staring slantways at the man. 'Not so I know of.'

'Very well.' The man blew on the photographs and put them back into his pocket. 'That was my wife.'

'Dead?' the boy asked.

Slowly the man shook his head. He pursed his lips as though about to whistle and answered in a long-drawn way: 'Nuuu –' he said. 'I will explain.'

The beer on the counter before the man was in a large brown mug. He did not pick it up to drink. Instead he bent down and, putting his face over the rim, he rested there for a moment. Then with both hands he tilted the mug and sipped.

'Some night you'll go to sleep with your big nose in a mug and drown,' said Leo. 'Prominent transient drowns in beer. That would be a cute death.'

The paper-boy tried to signal to Leo. While the man was not looking he screwed up his face and worked his mouth to question soundlessly: 'Drunk?' But Leo only raised his eyebrows and turned away to put some pink strips of bacon on the grill. The man pushed the mug away from him, straightened himself, and folded his loose crooked hands on the counter. His face was sad as he looked at the paper-boy. He did not blink, but from time to time the lids closed down with delicate gravity over his pale green eyes. It was nearing dawn and the boy shifted the weight of the paper-sack.

'I am talking about love,' the man said. 'With me it is a science.'

The boy half slid down from the stool. But the man raised his forefinger, and there was something about him that held the boy and would not let him go away.

'Twelve years ago I married the woman in the photograph. She was my wife for one year, nine months, three days, and two nights. I loved her. Yes . . .' He tightened his blurred, rambling voice and said again: 'I loved her. I thought also that she loved me. I was a railroad engineer. She had all home comforts and luxuries. It never crept into my brain that she was not satisfied. But do you know what happened?'

'Mgneeow!' said Leo.

The man did not take his eyes from the boy's face. 'She left me. I came in one night and the house was empty and she was gone. She left me.'

'With a fellow?' the boy asked.

Gently the man placed his palm down on the counter. 'Why naturally, Son. A woman does not run off like that alone.'

The café was quiet, the soft rain black and endless in the street outside. Leo pressed down the frying bacon with the prongs of his long fork. 'So you have been chasing the floozie for eleven years. You frazzled old rascal!'

For the first time the man glanced at Leo. 'Please don't be vulgar. Besides, I was not speaking to you.' He turned back to the boy and said in a trusting and secretive undertone: 'Let's not pay any attention to him. O.K.?'

The paper-boy nodded doubtfully.

'It was like this,' the man continued. 'I am a person who feels many things. All my life one thing after another has impressed me. Moonlight. The leg of a pretty girl. One thing after another. But the point is that when I had enjoyed anything there was a peculiar sensation as though it was laying around loose in me. Nothing seemed to finish itself up or fit in with the other things. Women? I had my portion of them. The same. Afterwards laying around loose in me. I was a man who had never loved.'

Very slowly he closed his eyelids, and the gesture was like a curtain drawn at the end of a scene in a play. When he spoke again his voice was excited and the words came fast – the lobes of his large, loose ears seemed to tremble.

'Then I met this woman. I was fifty-one years old and she always said she was thirty. I met her at a filling station and we were married within three days. And do you know what it was like? I just can't tell you. All I had ever felt was gathered together around this woman.

54

Nothing lay around loose in me any more but was finished up by her.'

The man stopped suddenly and stroked his long nose. His voice sank down to a steady and reproachful undertone: 'I'm not explaining this right. What happened was this. There were these beautiful feelings and loose little pleasures inside me. And this woman was something like an assembly line for my soul. I run these little pieces of myself through her and I come out complete. Now do you follow me?'

'What was her name?' the boy asked.

'Oh,' he said. 'I called her Dodo. But that is immaterial.'

'Did you try to make her come back?'

The man did not seem to hear. 'Under the circumstances you can imagine how I felt when she left me.'

Leo took the bacon from the grill and folded two strips of it between a bun. He had a grey face, with slitted eyes, and a pinched nose saddled by faint blue shadows. One of the mill workers signalled for more coffee and Leo poured it. He did not give refills on coffee free. The spinner ate breakfast there every morning, but the better Leo knew his customers the stingier he treated them. He nibbled his own bun as though he grudged it to himself.

'And you never got hold of her again?'

The boy did not know what to think of the man, and

his child's face was uncertain with mingled curiosity and doubt. He was new on the paper route; it was still strange to him to be out in the town in the black, queer early morning.

'Yes,' the man said. 'I took a number of steps to get her back. I went around trying to locate her. I went to Tulsa, where she had folks. And to Mobile. I went to every town she had ever mentioned to me, and I hunted down every man she had formerly been connected with. Tulsa, Atlanta, Chicago, Cheehaw, Memphis . . . For the better part of two years I chased around the country trying to lay hold of her.'

'But the pair of them had vanished from the face of the earth!' said Leo.

'Don't listen to him,' the man said confidentially. 'And also just forget those two years. They are not important. What matters is that around the third year a curious thing began to happen to me.'

'What?' the boy asked.

The man leaned down and tilted his mug to take a sip of beer. But as he hovered over the mug his nostrils fluttered slightly; he sniffed the staleness of the beer and did not drink. 'Love is a curious thing to begin with. At first I thought only of getting her back. It was a kind of mania. But then as time went on I tried to remember her. But do you know what happened?'

'No,' the boy said.

'When I laid myself down on a bed and tried to think about her my mind became a blank. I couldn't see her. I would take out her pictures and look. No good. Nothing doing. A blank. Can you imagine it?'

'Say, Mac!' Leo called down the counter. 'Can you imagine this bozo's mind a blank!'

Slowly, as though fanning away flies, the man waved his hand. His green eyes were concentrated and fixed on the shallow little face of the paper-boy.

'But a sudden piece of glass on a sidewalk. Or a nickel tune in a music box. A shadow on a wall at night. And I would remember. It might happen in a street and I would cry or bang my head against a lamp-post. You follow me?'

'A piece of glass . . .' the boy said.

'Anything. I would walk around and I had no power of how and when to remember her. You think you can put up a kind of shield. But remembering don't come to a man face forward – it corners around sideways. I was at the mercy of everything I saw and heard. Suddenly instead of me combing the countryside to find her she began to chase me around in my very soul. *She* chasing *me*, mind you! And in my soul.'

The boy asked finally: 'What part of the country were you in then?'

'Ooh,' the man groaned. 'I was a sick mortal. It was like smallpox. I confess, Son, that I boozed. I fornicated. I committed any sin that suddenly appealed to me. I am loathe to confess it, but I will do so. When I recall that period it is all curdled in my mind, it was so terrible.'

The man leaned his head down and tapped his forehead on the counter. For a few seconds he stayed bowed over in this position, the back of his stringy neck covered with orange furze, his hands with their long warped fingers held palm to palm in an attitude of prayer. Then the man straightened himself; he was smiling and suddenly his face was bright and tremulous and old.

'It was in the fifth year that it happened,' he said. 'And with it I started my science.'

Leo's mouth jerked with a pale, quick grin. 'Well none of we boys are getting any younger,' he said. Then with sudden anger he balled up a dish-cloth he was holding and threw it down hard on the floor. 'You draggle-tailed old Romeo!'

'What happened?' the boy asked.

The old man's voice was high and clear: 'Peace,' he answered.

'Huh?'

'It is hard to explain scientifically, Son,' he said. 'I guess the logical explanation is that she and I had fleed around from each other for so long that finally we just got tangled up together and lay down and quit. Peace. A queer and beautiful blankness. It was spring in Portland and the rain came every afternoon. All evening I just stayed there on my bed in the dark. And that is how the science come to me.'

The windows in the streetcar were pale blue with light. The two soldiers paid for their beers and opened the door – one of the soldiers combed his hair and wiped off his muddy puttees before they went outside. The three mill workers bent silently over their breakfasts. Leo's clock was ticking on the wall.

'It is this. And listen carefully. I meditated on love and reasoned it out. I realized what is wrong with us. Men fall in love for the first time. And what do they fall in love with?'

The boy's soft mouth was partly open and he did not answer.

'A woman,' the old man said. 'Without science, with nothing to go by, they undertake the most dangerous and sacred experience on God's earth. They fall in love with a woman. Is that correct, Son?'

'Yeah,' the boy said faintly.

'They start at the wrong end of love. They begin at the climax. Can you wonder it is so miserable? Do you know how men should love?'

The old man reached over and grasped the boy by

59

the collar of his leather jacket. He gave him a gentle little shake and his green eyes gazed down unblinking and grave.

'Son, do you know how love should be begun?'

The boy sat small and listening and still. Slowly he shook his head. The old man leaned closer and whispered:

'A tree. A rock. A cloud.'

It was still raining outside in the street: a mild, grey, endless rain. The mill whistle blew for the six o'clock shift and the three spinners paid and went away. There was no one in the café but Leo, the old man, and the little paper-boy.

'The weather was like this in Portland,' he said. 'At the time my science was begun. I meditated and I started very cautious. I would pick up something from the street and take it home with me. I bought a goldfish and I concentrated on the goldfish and I loved it. I graduated from one thing to another. Day by day I was getting this technique. On the road from Portland to San Diego –'

'Aw shut up!' screamed Leo suddenly. 'Shut up! Shut up!'

The old man still held the collar of the boy's jacket; he was trembling and his face was earnest and bright and wild. 'For six years now I have gone around by myself and built up my science. And now I am a master.

Son. I can love anything. No longer do I have to think about it even. I see a street full of people and a beautiful light comes in me. I watch a bird in the sky. Or I meet a traveller on the road. Everything, Son. And anybody. All stranger and all loved! Do you realize what a science like mine can mean?'

The boy held himself stiffly, his hands curled tight around the counter edge. Finally he asked: 'Did you ever really find that lady?'

'What? What say, Son?'

'I mean,' the boy asked timidly. 'Have you fallen in love with a woman again?'

The old man loosened his grasp on the boy's collar. He had turned away and for the first time his green eyes had a vague and scattered look. He lifted the mug from the counter, drank down the yellow beer. His head was shaking slowly from side to side. Then finally he answered: 'No, Son. You see that is the last step in my science. I go cautious. And I am not quite ready yet.'

'Well!' said Leo. 'Well, well, well!'

The old man stood in the open doorway. 'Remember,' he said. Framed there in the grey damp light of the early morning he looked shrunken and seedy and frail. But his smile was bright. 'Remember I love you,' he said with a last nod. And the door closed quietly behind him.

The boy did not speak for a long time. He pulled down the bangs on his forehead and slid his grimy little forefinger around the rim of his empty cup. Then without looking at Leo he finally asked:

'Was he drunk?'

'No,' said Leo shortly.

The boy raised his clear voice higher. 'Then was he a dope fiend?'

'No.'

The boy looked up at Leo, and his flat little face was desperate, his voice urgent and shrill. 'Was he crazy? Do you think he was a lunatic?' The paper-boy's voice dropped suddenly with doubt. 'Leo? Or not?'

But Leo would not answer him. Leo had run a night café for fourteen years, and he held himself to be a critic of craziness. There were the town characters and also the transients who roamed in from the night. He knew the manias of all of them. But he did not want to satisfy the questions of the waiting child. He tightened his pale face and was silent.

So the boy pulled down the right flap of his helmet and as he turned to leave he made the only comment that seemed safe to him, the only remark that could not be laughed down and despised:

'He sure has done a lot of travelling.'

a little history

Penguin Modern Classics were launched in 1961, and have been shaping the reading habits of generations ever since.

The list began with distinctive grey spines and evocative pictorial covers – a look that, after various incarnations, continues to influence their current design – and with books that are still considered landmark classics today.

Penguin Modern Classics have caused scandal and political change, inspired great films and broken down barriers, whether social, sexual or the boundaries of language itself. They remain the most provocative, groundbreaking, exciting and revolutionary works of the last 100 years (or so).

In 2011, on the fiftieth anniversary of the Modern Classics, we're publishing fifty Mini Modern Classics: the very best short fiction by writers ranging from Beckett to Conrad, Nabokov to Saki, Updike to Wodehouse. Though they don't take long to read, they'll stay with you long after you turn the final page.

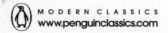

MODERN CLASSICS
www.penguinclassics.com